I0520342

GULITH
New York

The Cosmic Deflector

Stanton A. Coblentz

Copyright © 2024 by GULITH New York

All rights reserved. No part of this publication may be reproduced or transmitted in any form or by any means electronic or mechanical, including information storage and retrieval systems without permission in writing from the publisher, except for student research using the appropriate citations.

ISBN: 978-1-63652-327-9

THE
COSMIC
DEFLECTOR

STANTON A. COBLENTZ

His face red with haste, and his blue eyes glittering, Dan Holcomb burst into the laboratory.

"Just look at this, Lucile!" he cried, flinging his hat halfway across the room, and almost dancing in his joy. "Lord! Look at this, will you!"

Lucile Travers glanced up from her Bunsen burner, and stared in surprise at Dan's six-foot bulk. She was used to her lover's flaming enthusiasms; but never had she seen him so beside himself. How boyish he seemed, with his lean, keen, studious face, and eyes that were all a blaze of youthful delight!

"There! Take a peep at that, old girl!" he rushed on, as he snapped out his wallet and displayed a handsomely embossed letter.

Her eyes popped half out of her head as she glanced at the sheet. "Twenty-five—twenty-five thousand dollars, Dan!" she gasped. "Why, it—it can't be real!"

"But it *is* real! Boy! this isn't any pipe dream, believe me! A neat twenty-five thousand—that's what I'm offered for my Deflector!"

While she stared at him dazedly, he did an impromptu hop, skip and jump. She did not need to be told about the Cosmic Deflector— had she not been at Dan's side during these many months when he had worked at it? Had she not shared his enthusiasm at the Gravitational Ray Theory?—the idea that gravity was due to an invisible ray shot out by the electrons and hence was akin to electricity in its origin? Had she not believed, with him, that this ray formed a current, which, like electricity, could be bent, or twisted from its course? Had she not glowed at the discovery of the telurium compound—telurox, they called it—which, on burning, would send out beams that diverted the rays of gravity? And had they not, poring together over his plans, decided that it would be possible to alter the movements of the very planets?

All this was in the girl's mind as her eyes raced along the lines of that incredible letter. It was from Hogarth, Wiley and Malvine, a well known firm of construction engineers. And there was no doubt that it actually did offer $25,000!—$25,000 for all rights in the Deflector, along with Dan's services for a year!

"Who'd have thought it?" enthused the inventor. "Why, Bert Wilcox—you know, my old college chum—introduced me to Wiley only last Tuesday, and told about the Deflector. When Wiley asked me to lay the plans before him, I didn't imagine—"

He rambled on for a minute, then broke short. "But good heavens, Lucy, let's forget all that! It's not the Deflector I want to think about! It's you! You, Lucy! Don't you see? Our waiting—it's over now!"

She did indeed see. For three years they had been engaged, almost since the day when they had met as laboratory assistants here at Columbia Chemicals. But Dan, saddled with the care of his aged parents, had seen no way out of a financial morass that might mean further years of waiting.

Down from her vivid brown eyes and over her lovely face the tears were streaming as his strong arms gathered about her and she pressed close to him in confidence and love.

Yet why was it that, even in this moment of their triumph, a gnawing suspicion crept over her, chilling her joy with a dull clutching uneasiness?

There was a look of steel-and-granite on Dan's ordinarily cheerful face as he came striding home. He had only a wan smile for his bride of three months as she greeted him at the door of their little apartment.

"Don't mind me, Lucy, if I act like a man with his last penny gone," he explained, after a moment. "It's those damned fellows Hogarth, Wiley and Malvine. Well, you know I've suspected they weren't all above board."

"What's the trouble now?"

He came close to her, and she noticed how red his face was, and how his arms trembled.

"They're worse than Hitler, that's what the trouble is! Want to make me their stooge, the crawling worms!"

He took a turn or two about the room, then went on, more composedly.

"Remember how I agreed to use the Deflector to pull the earth a few thousand miles off its course—only a few thousand, for experimental purposes! Well, now it's more than that distance off, and getting further every minute. This afternoon I put it up to them that we'd better send things into reverse. What do you think they did? Laughed at me!"

"I don't call it exactly a laughing matter."

"Believe me, it's not! That fellow Wiley came up, with his horse-like face and black eyes that seemed to drill right into me. 'Listen here, old boy,' he said. 'I'll let you into a secret. We haven't any idea of putting the earth back on its orbit—not just yet! We'll let the distance widen a few million miles. We're going to raise hell on this planet—simply hell!'"

"My glory, is he crazy?"

"Not by a long shot! That's the terrible part of it. They outlined their scheme to me—enough, anyhow, to show it's the most diabolical plot ever hatched. Thought I would work with them. 'Never fear, you'll get your share of the swag, old fellow!' Wiley promised. What does he take me for—a louse?"

The vivid blue flames of his anger seemed to leap straight out of Dan's eyes.

"Well, what is their plot?"

"To steal the planet—make themselves a World Triumvirate, the dirty cutthroats! Their scheme is clever too, clever as the devil!"

By degrees he explained the conspiracy, so far as he knew it. Wiley and his colleagues intended to deflect five or ten per cent of the sun's gravity, so sending the earth several million miles farther into space. This would not be fatal, but would cause great climatic inconveniences, and would so alarm the whole world that it would pay any price to get back on its orbit. By that time the agents of the Triumvirate would be planted in every country—Quislings of the sort that can always be bribed by the prospect of a little power, a little notoriety. When the present national leaders had been frightened out of their wits, they would be willing, even eager to turn over the reins to the Triumvirate "for the duration of the emergency," in the belief that Hogarth and his fellows would save the earth. Meanwhile the Triumvirs would establish a secret police. They would demand control of the armies, navies and air fleets of the earth. And they would win reputations as wizards who had rescued the globe—and so would gain popular support everywhere. By the time the planet was back in its proper orbit they would have it, literally, in the palms of their hands.

"Even if they didn't tell me all the details," Dan finished, "I could guess what they left unsaid. Fact is, they're nothing but a gang of hijackers, saying 'Your money or your life!' to the whole world. The worst of it is, they'll have us all in such an infernal hole that it'll be too late unless we act darned soon!"

"What surprises me," meditated Lucile, "is that they should take you into their confidence."

"Probably they didn't doubt my loyalty, after the way I've worked with them all these months. Besides, that fellow Hogarth made a remark I didn't like. Turning that beefy red face of his toward me, with a wicked twinkle in his racoon-like eyes, he said, 'The man who works with us,

Holcomb, will have power and glory. But the man who works against us will be—underground!"

There was a look of terror on Lucile's face as Dan went on, "Naturally, I made out to be on their side. Hope to heaven they weren't able to see through me!"

The smell of burning, from the direction of the kitchen, offered Lucile temporary diversion. And when she had returned from her scorched dinner pots, Dan had come to his decision.

"Only one thing to do, Lucy! I'll go to the police at once. If they act in time—well, maybe they'll still save the world."

Already he had seized his hat, and was halfway to the door.

"For mercy's sake, be careful!" she pleaded, distracted.

"Don't you worry, I'll do my best. Wait here for me, Lucy. I'll be back in half an hour."

Despite her appeals, he was already halfway into the outer hall. She was never to forget the brave, tragical look of his grimly set face. She knew that she could not hold him back; that she had no right to hold him back. Yet something seemed to rise up in her throat and choke her as the door slammed and she knew that he was gone.

A deep depression had settled over her when the specified half hour had passed and he had not returned. When the half hour had lengthened into an hour, uneasiness gave place to alarm. When an hour had been extended to two, alarm rose to terror. At last, after two hours, her dread got the better of her and she telephoned the police.

No! there had been no accident to a Daniel Holcomb! No! he had not come to the station that evening! No, sorry, but they could not send out detectives to investigate! "Don't think there's any need of that, Ma'am," the sergeant finished. "Chances are he met some old pal and went off for a drink, and just forgot the time."

But Lucile, as she put down the receiver, knew that Dan had not "gone off for a drink." Realizing that he had not even reached the station, she understood that her gravest misgivings had been justified. And then it was that, for the first time, she broke down and wept.

Probably no one who lived through the summer of 1977 will forget the consternation, the terror that convulsed the planet. It was in late May when astronomers reported unforeseen perturbations in the earth's orbit; and by early June it had been officially confirmed that we were off our proper path in space. At first the variation was slight—a mere few thousand miles. But with the passage of weeks, our distance from the sun widened until the earth was off its course by a million, two million, five million miles!

No hypothesis put forth by science could explain the occurrence. It was suggested that some dead, dark sun, from the depths of space, had caught our world in its gravitational pull. But in that case, would it not also have affected Mars, Jupiter, and the other planets? Yet these, except for minute variations ascribable to the earth's altered position, were unaffected!

But few persons, those desperate days, cared much about the theory behind the event. What concerned them was the peril to their own existence. Already the disturbances were acute. By mid-July, New York and London shivered in snow flurries; the frost had ruined agriculture in half the north temperate regions; while in the Argentine and South Africa, which were now experiencing their winter, hundreds of thousands were freezing to death. Meanwhile blizzards and tornadoes swept the globe; tidal waves, earthquakes and volcanic eruptions testified to the upset of the age-old equilibrium; while thunder storms of unexampled severity, floods, and meteoric displays of a brilliance never known before, added to the protests of the elements and the terror of the people.

Long before the summer was over, men began to resign themselves to the idea that life on earth was near its end. For, not only were we receiving less solar radiation than formerly, but the years and therefore the seasons were being lengthened; hence the winters would be unendurably severe. As we drifted ever farther into space, an unlifting frost would settle over every portion of the globe, including the tropics; and life, frozen and starved, would disappear.

It was on July 15 that the world was electrified by an announcement appearing in newspapers throughout the world. A celebrated firm of construction engineers, Hogarth, Wiley and Malvine, had not only discovered the root of the trouble but had contrived a way to cure it. However, they would need the cooperation of every man, woman and child on earth; they must be given control of all the world's resources, of all mines, power-plants, factories, and systems of transportation, in order to throw everything that mankind possessed into the battle.

At any other time, such a proposal would have been laughed to scorn. But now, when the world's nerves were stretched taut with terror, men were eager to clutch at any straw. A committee of alleged experts (who, it subsequently turned out, were in the pay of Hogarth and Company) endorsed the claims of the self-styled saviors of the world; legislative groups, likewise in their pay, voted them unlimited power; dictators and presidents, in despair, gave them the right of way over great nations. But what did this matter? What did anything matter, except that Earth be saved from destruction?

In a concrete-walled, electrically lighted basement chamber, originally intended as a storeroom, a prisoner stalked restlessly. Up and down, up and down, up and down the ten-by-twelve windowless space he wandered. His eyes were bloodshot; his fingers twitched uneasily; his rumpled clothes bore the signs of a recent struggle. At one side of the room, on a rude work-bench, some food and water stood untouched. From outside the closed doors, he could hear the obscene jests exchanged by two armed guards.

His mind reeled as he recalled the events of the past few hours; how three men, amid the fogs of twilight, had surrounded him as he emerged from the apartment house to go for the police; how one of them had clapped a gag over his mouth, and the other two had forced him into a waiting sedan.... So swiftly had it all happened that he could hardly piece together the successive steps of the crime in logical order.

Yet that the deed had been ordered by his former employers was manifest. His horror at their plans had been evident, much as he had tried to conceal it! Their secret police were already functioning! Undoubtedly one of them, eavesdropping at the door of his apartment, had overheard his remarks to his wife, which he had made little effort to subdue. And now that he was in the enemy's power, he would have no chance to thwart or reveal their schemes!

Contemplatively he gazed about his jail. Bare walls! a bare floor! Not a tool by which he might attempt to escape! The prisoner felt in his pockets—even his knife had been taken from him. He thought of his wife—and knew that she would be growing frantic. Yet, though he realized that the odds against him were thousands to one, he would not let himself despair. For a long while he leaned meditatively against a wall, his brows wrinkled, his glance withdrawn, as he pondered, pondered over ways and means to surmount his barriers. For upon his escape, he knew, the world's freedom depended.

It was with the air of a beaten dog that, one afternoon in early August, Hogarth came slouching into his mahogany-paneled headquarters in the twenty-two-story office building he had recently appropriated.

As July turned into August, the earth's movements had become more erratic than ever. Even to the naked eye, the sun's disk had grown appreciably smaller. The Antarctic cold had begun to lay a white blanket over jungles beneath the Equator; while already the trees of the eastern United States had taken on the hues of October. No one who lived through those disconsolate days will forget the tragic aspect of our cities: thoroughfares almost deserted, and only an occasional business house still open; a handful of people passing, with wan features and drooping heads; and only one question on any one's lips, "When, when will it end?"

With the haste of panic, Hogarth, Wiley and Malvine had been granted everything they asked. They had been placed in control of all natural resources, all factories and railways, all armies and navies. They had been given *carte blanche* with the earth. All other rulers took orders from them. They were, as they had aimed to be, universal dictators. This tremendous power had been granted them, so that they might save us all, as they had promised. Then why did they not save us? men asked, chattering with cold and terror.

They might have had their answer had they seen Hogarth sagging into his office on that August afternoon. Rubbing his fleshy red face with an equally fleshy red hand, he dropped into a seat, and grumbled, "Guess it's no use, boys! Simply don't seem able to turn the trick!"

Wiley had leaped to his feet. His horse-like teeth were unbared beneath curling lips. "God! Mean to say she won't work?"

"No, blast it, she won't," concurred Malvine, who had come in just behind Hogarth. "Haven't the two of us been slaving like teamsters, along with McBride and a whole army of engineers? That cursed Deflector has gone haywire! Why, I'll swear we diverted gravity enough to pull the earth halfway over to Venus. And what are the results? Nil. Precisely nil!"

Wiley stood regarding his fellow plotters in silence. An unpleasant smirk formed itself upon his lips.

"Well, don't worry, boys. In the long run, a day or two more or less won't matter."

"No, I'll be cursed if it will!" growled Hogarth. "Nothing in hell will matter if we die along with everybody else!"

Wiley gasped. "What makes you so damned cheerful?"

"Well, how we going to save ourselves? I'm putting it to you straight, old man. What if we are world dictators? We're doomed like every beetle and rat on this crazy planet. The whole rotten globe is going to freeze!"

"Afraid that's so," agreed Malvine, with a wry puckering of his long, fox-like face. "We've tried hard enough, but we've about shot our bolt. Frankly, there isn't any known principle by which we can get the Deflector working again."

For the first time, a pallor had come across Wiley's features. He was the scheming brains of the firm, but had not kept up on his science, and always took his colleagues' word on technical matters.

For a while, he remained silent, his saturnine face grave with thought. "By thunder," he finally broke out, "I'm not going to let myself die just yet—not when I've got the world in my hands! There's one man who'll be able to help out with that damned Deflector."

"Who's your genius?" sneered Malvine.

"Well, who but this fellow Holcomb?"

"Holcomb?"

"Of course. He's harmless now—but useless—in his underground storeroom. I'm for taking him out—under proper supervision. He'll know how to use the Deflector, if any man does!"

Hogarth's gloom relaxed a bit. "Good!" he approved. "Can't do any harm to try. We've got to make damned sure, though, he doesn't get loose or communicate with his friends. I'd a thousand times rather shoot him like a yellow dog!"

Wiley chuckled; and the hands of all three conspirators shot out in agreement.

Dan's face was pale after his long confinement. His cheeks were sunken, and had the smoldering look of deep suffering. But there was scorn in his manner as he faced his persecutors.

"Yes, that's the story," Wiley was reiterating. "Guess we're not quite on to the ropes. If you'll work a little at the Deflector—"

Dan glared at his tormentors, his eyes kindled with a fierce blue glitter. His chin was outthrust, but his manner was quiet as he replied, after a moment's hesitation, "Show me to the laboratory!"

Wiley arose, and prepared to lead the way.

"We'll give you one week!" he stipulated. "Exactly one week! By then, we'll expect you to show results!"

After being escorted blindfolded to a secret laboratory, Dan labored incessantly. He would pretend to obey the Triumvirs, while actually doing all he could to oppose them! But in the beginning, he had to confess to himself, his position looked nearly hopeless. Eagerly he searched for some possible means of escape—some way of signalling the outside world. But two armed guards stood watching just beyond the only door.

His most pressing thought was to get word to his wife—not only to relieve her terrible anxiety, but to plot with her his escape. He had, naturally, been denied access to a telephone; yet he would not let this balk him. Deftly making use of the electrical gear and headphones of a half dismantled shortwave radio receiver which he had found in the laboratory, he set about to tap the wires in a remote corner where, he noted, a telephone connection had formerly been. Meanwhile he was careful to keep as wide a distance as possible between him and the guards.

To prevent them from hearing his voice when he had tapped the wire, he set a particularly noisy motor in operation close to the door. Then, trembling with eagerness, he spoke through his improvised speaking apparatus. To his delight, he heard an answering, "Number, please!" His tones were jerky with excitement as he gave his home number. But, a moment later, his joy froze within him.

Across the wire there came a sickening, "The line has been disconnected, sir!" And in response to his quavering inquiry, all he could get was, "No, sir, they mentioned no other number to call."

He was just about to give another number—that of a friend who might be able to supply information about Lucile—when he felt a heavy hand on one shoulder, and looked up into the angry eyes of his guards.

"None of that, young man!" bawled one jailer, while the other snatched up the telephone equipment. "I thought you were up to some mischief! Get back to work!"

Two rubber truncheons came down upon Dan's defenseless flesh as, with a groan, he struggled back to his bench.

As late August shivered toward September, the world's state became still more terrifying. Whirlwinds rushed more severely than ever through the darkening skies; blizzards raged, and a mantle of white covered the northern United States; agriculture and industry had virtually ceased; and men passed their time in mumbling prayers, in making wild, fruitless studies of the heavens, and in the sodden forgetfulness of dissipation.

Dan, however, knew nothing of all this as he labored in his hidden laboratory. Working once more at the Deflector, in the desire to save the earth from freezing, he had made a discovery—one which, as he toiled, had darkened his face with lines of discouragement that gradually gave place to horror. And in the end he had sagged down, exhausted, with bloodshot eyes and drooping limbs ... oppressed with a nightmare realization.

During the weeks of his imprisonment, the earth had moved millions of miles farther from the sun. And the strength of telurox, lessening with the inverse square of the distance, was insufficient to cover the gap. It was beyond his power to make up the difference. Unless a miracle intervened, the earth was doomed!

Nevertheless, was there not just the remotest hope?—possibly a chance in a million? If only he could gain control of a larger laboratory, with capable assistants, he might try a certain newly conceived experiment. But to ask his captors to provide such a laboratory would be to put himself and the earth even more hopelessly in their power.

Instead, his thoughts kept wandering in another direction. If he could once get into touch with his wife, she might be able to help him! But where was she now? Somewhere in hiding? Or imprisoned by the Triumvirs? Yet if she were still at liberty, was there not a means by which he might still communicate with her? He recalled how, during their years together at Columbia Chemicals, they had worked out a secret code, by which they could tap out love messages on the walls. Could this code not be used over the radio? Could he not transmit signals over various wave-lengths, so that sooner or later—if she still listened to the radio—she would recognize his message?

At any rate, he would try. Hoping to ward off suspicion, he pretended to work at a Cosmic Deflector which, telescope-shaped and two feet in thickness, reached from floor to ceiling. Within this great tube he concealed a small radio transmitter which he had hastily contrived, out of the abundant electrical equipment of the Deflector. Its power, he knew, would be limited, but it could be heard well enough locally. By means of a device resembling an electric bell, he was able to transmit signals, on a dot and dash system. So rapidly did he work that, after a few hours, this novel broadcaster was sending out its rat-tat-tat.

His next step was to repair the half dismantled radio receiver. This task completed, he began to tap out signals, "Lucile! Lucile! Hear me! I am imprisoned by the Triumvirs! Follow my directions, and we may still save the world!"

Time after time—hundreds of times—he repeated this message. Was he but playing a fool's game? So he asked himself as the hours stretched out; as the days dragged past and still no answer came. Was he not wasting his efforts while the earth whirled to its doom?

It was on the fourth day of the experiment. Pale with anxiety and fatigue, Dan still tapped out his messages; still listened at the radio. Suddenly he stood up, with a start. What was that sound he heard? That answering tap, tap, tap? Three shorts and a long—three shorts and a long! In their code, what did that mean? "Where are you? Tell me, where are you?" Or had he counted the signals wrongly. In desperate eagerness, he stood listening. Now there came two longs and a short; then a short and two longs—

"Well, old man, how's the work going?"

Dan was so shocked that he leapt back several feet. Not more than a yard away, leering with a horse-like grin, was the face of Wiley! And just in the background, devilishly gaping, were Hogarth and Malvine.

Dan's first thought was that the enemy knew what he was about, and had come to mock him at the moment of his seeming success.

"Well, how's she going?" Wiley reiterated. "Any progress?"

With an effort, Dan snapped out of his stupefied silence. "Oh, she's promising very well," he managed to say.

Through the radio, with maddening insistency, came the rat-tat-tat of a message. It was impossible, under the circumstances, to record or translate it! The thought flashed over Dan that he had been tricked; that the message came from the Triumvirs, who were now enjoying his discomfiture!

"What's that damned noise?" Hogarth demanded, as if to lend confirmation to this theory.

Reaching for a secret switch, Dan snapped off the radio. Only a clever bluff, he knew, could save him now!

"Oh, it's only the magnified sound of the impact of the gravitational rays upon the Deflector," he lied, glibly, still hoping against hope. "In other words, the vibrational impetus of—"

"To hell with your long-winded explanations!" Wiley cut him short, impatiently. "What we want to know is, what progress have you made? Any sign of getting the earth back in place?"

"Time we gave you is about up!" said Malvine. "If you're not getting results, better turn things over to some one else!"

"Everything's in the devil's own mess!" sighed Hogarth. "It's hell on earth—people freezing to death right and left. By God! if I thought you weren't getting somewhere, I'd have you choked to death, just for the fun of it!"

"Well, as a matter of fact," fabricated Dan, "the Super-Detectonic rays are a bit slow in getting into operation. But you can't expect miracles. If you'll give me a little more time—a few more days, maybe a week—I'll promise you results."

A cold sweat had broken out all over him before he had explained, in scientific detail, just why he might succeed if given another week. Thank God! they had not suspected! Or had they suspected?—and were they only toying with him? In any case, they had, wittingly or unwittingly, broken into his experiment at the crucial point. Would he ever again catch the interrupted message?

His fingers shaking with eagerness, he turned back to the radio. But even as he did so, the sneer on Wiley's retreating face hit him like a taunt.

After the first cruel shock, Lucile had realized just what was behind Dan's disappearance. She not only was sure that he had been kidnapped by Hogarth and his gang, but that any effort on her part to report to the police would result in her own immediate apprehension. Already her position was perilous—might the conspirators not finish the job by seizing her at any moment? There was nothing to be done, therefore, except to change her residence, without informing anyone where she was going. Then, in secret, she might plan to free her husband.

At first, however, no tenable idea came to her. Meanwhile, through her old professors at Merlin University, where she had been an excellent student, she obtained access to the chemical laboratory, and experimented day and night for means to increase the power of telurox. If it were possible to divert to the earth enough of the gravity that shot past it into space, might the planet not even now be drawn back to its orbit?

For weeks she labored, without results. She was merely one more discouraged person in a discouraged world, when at length a startling incident occurred. She had gone out for a hasty bite of lunch, and on her return she noticed that her assistant, young Dick Harson, was listening to the radio, as he often did, while munching at a sandwich.

"Well, anything new?" she asked, with a faint smile.

"Nothing but a crazy noise, like a telegrapher breaking in on the broadcast," he answered. "If it's still on, I'll show you."

He switched the dial. "There it is!" he exclaimed, after a moment. "Doesn't it sound just like a secret code?"

At first she listened indifferently, her mind preoccupied; then gave a start, for she recognized something astoundingly familiar. Surely, it was but an accident! It must be an accident that the succession of long and short syllables made sense, according to her old code with Dan! "Imprisoned by the Triumvirs! Follow my directions, and we may still save the world."

Harson was astonished to see how eagerly the young woman sprang from her seat; and how she stood staring, as if she had seen a ghost.

With the frenzy of a famished person finding food, she bent down to listen. For a minute she remained there, leaning over the radio with a puzzled look, as if she could not quite make out the message. Then, to Harson's still greater amazement, she dashed to the laboratory's short wave transmitter, and, beating together two bits of metal, began to send out a series of long and short sounds, similar to the signals they had heard.

By this time the rat-tat-tat from the other end had ceased. It was more than half an hour later, when she had paused to rest momentarily, that fresh signals came over the radio. A flood of tears rushed to her eyes as she made out the words, "Lucile! Lucile—it is I!"

"Take this down, Lucy! Bismuth tetrachloride in combination with the borium salt I just mentioned will have a catalyzing effect on telurox, increasing its activity fifty per cent—more than enough to bring the earth back to its orbit. So my experiments indicate. Try it out just as soon as possible!"

Such was one of the first messages that Dan tapped out to his wife, after a few explanatory interchanges.

"For God's sake, hurry! At any minute those bandits may catch on!" the message continued. "Let me hear the results as soon as you can! We've just got to succeed, and trap them!"

Several days went by, while the signals still flashed back and forth. But Dan knew, as did Lucile also, that their time was short, very short. All too soon the week allowed him by Hogarth, Wiley and Malvine passed; all too soon the sinister three paid him another visit.

They found him still working at the Deflector, from whose interior once more a strange rat-tat-tat was issuing.

"Well," demanded Hogarth, "what success?"

Dan looked up casually. "Oh," he declared, trying to appear unconcerned, "as much as could be expected."

"What the devil does that mean?" snapped Wiley, projecting his ridged horse-face pugnaciously. "You promised results in a week. Have you had them? Can you put the earth back on its orbit?"

"If you'll give me more time—"

"More time, and we'll all be driven to our deaths!" stormed Malvine. "Not another day! No, not another hour!"

Wiley, who had been peering into the recesses of the Deflector, was fumbling in an exploratory fashion at its fittings. Suddenly he pulled a half concealed lever, released a panel, and let out a low whistle. "What in blazes is this?"

With an angry wrench, he drew out a mass of wires, bulbs and batteries. "Looks to me like a radio transmitter!" he growled.

All three men glared menace at Dan. He had foreseen and dreaded this very event. Confronted with the evidence, it would be folly to attempt a denial. His only course would be to try to turn suspicion in the least dangerous channel.

"Of course it's a radio transmitter," he admitted, quietly. "I'll be frank with you—I was hoping to find a chance to get away."

Ominously the three conspirators closed about him. There was a nasty rumble in Wiley's voice as he decided. "Well then, you damned traitor, it's up to us to put you where you won't get away—not for many a good long day! We were cursed fools to place any trust in you!"

Abruptly he motioned to the guards. "Solitary confinement again— and a bread and water diet!" he barked. "Maybe that'll bring him around to reason!"

But even as Dan, bound and handcuffed, was being dragged off, he had grim satisfaction in reflecting that his persecutors could not guess the real purpose of his radio.

By the first of September, the earth was farther off its course than ever. Eleven million, twelve million, thirteen million miles! And every day the distance widened. Would its orbit, like that of a periodic comet, be lengthened into a long ellipse, taking it into the unthinkable cold beyond Jupiter or Saturn?

This was the question in every one's mind, when on September 2 a full-page advertisement appeared in America's leading papers: "$50,000

Reward! For invention to counteract the Cosmic Deflector! All reasonable propositions given immediate personal attention. Hogarth, Wiley and Malvine."

It was on the never-to-be-forgotten third of September that the advertisers received their first applicant for the award. It was a young woman, of sad and earnest appearance; and the clerk who questioned her, perceiving that she had extraordinary information to offer, lost no time about summoning Hogarth.

"My name is Landers—Mary Landers," she introduced herself. "I was a laboratory assistant of Daniel Holcomb when he invented telurox. I have been trying to increase its power, and have had remarkable success. In fact, I come to claim that fifty thousand."

Hogarth gasped.

The caller went on to explain how, as a result of a long series of computations, she had mixed a small quantity of a certain bismuth salt with the telurox; and how this had increased its activity by more than fifty per cent. Fortunately, a huge Deflector had already been set up in the laboratory, for experimental purposes.

"Have you taken any observations today?" she finished. "If so, perhaps you've noticed that the earth is fifty thousand miles nearer the sun than yesterday."

"By glory!" exclaimed Hogarth. "That's just what Lasson Observatory reported, but I thought those fellows were all soused. Let's see! Got a model machine to show me?"

"Everything's over at Merlin University. If you'll just step into your car, we'll be there in twenty minutes."

"You bet I will!" agreed Hogarth eagerly, as he reached for his hat. "No harm looking at it!"

The young woman started toward the door; then turned back, as if on an after-thought. "Oh, by the way, don't your partners want to join us? I'd like to give a real demonstration, which it would waste a lot of good time and energy to repeat."

"Don't see what they've got on hand more important," muttered Hogarth. "Wait a minute."

From an adjoining room she could hear Hogarth's voice rising disputatiously. "No harm investigating, anyhow!" And she could not keep back a secret exultation when, after a time, he appeared in company with two men whom he introduced as "Mr. Wiley" and "Mr. Malvine."

Half an hour later, she had led them into the University laboratory, a corner of which had been partitioned off. There a twenty-four-inch telescope-like tube shot up through the ceiling; while nearer at hand was a table covered with complicated electrical devices.

"Well, trot out your discoveries!" barked Wiley.

From a compartment Miss Landers drew three pairs of binoculars, with wires attached. "Adjust these, gentlemen," she instructed.

Automatically each man reached for a pair. And as they took them, a look of triumph crossed the woman's averted face. She pressed a button— and with what astonishing results!

Her finger sought the button behind her; found it...

All three men gasped, and began to writhe. A convulsive shudder shot through each; they sagged, and fell to the floor; then gradually all three stiffened, except for their necks and faces, which still twitched spasmodically.

At the same time, the young woman pressed a buzzer; and three men, in the uniforms of university guards, hastened in with ropes, which they wound around the helpless trio.

"What—what in hell's name is this?" sputtered Wiley, as he began to recover from the first shock. "We—we're paralyzed!"

"That's just it," stated the lady, calmly. "You're paralyzed, from the necks down. I merely wanted to introduce you to another little invention of your friend Dan Holcomb. He asked me to show it to you, with his compliments. You see, the rays of telurox, much diluted and carried over a wire, will temporarily paralyze the human nerve centers. But have no fear. The spell will wear off in half an hour."

"This—this is an outrage!" groaned Hogarth, as he lay amid his ropes.

"Not at all. I'm sure, when you're no longer paralyzed, you won't mind signing a little paper, containing an order for the release of Mr. Holcomb—"

"What the devil makes you so interested in Holcomb?" flared back Wiley.

"Well, it's only that I happen to be his wife. Mary Landers is the name of a cousin of mine. Dan and I have been planning to get him out of your dungeon when you locked him up there again, as we expected you would. I'm simply carrying out his ideas."

Angry sounds, like the growls of enraged bears, came from the throats of all three prisoners.

"If we sign," demanded Malvine, "will you let us go?"

"There's only one promise I can make. If you don't sign, my friends here"—she designated the three guards—"will see that you remain paralyzed."

The conspirators were trapped, and they knew it; were caught like rats in a corner, beyond rescue by the corrupt system they had built up. And so, after their paralysis had begun to wear off and they had been re-paralyzed several times in succession, they bowed their heads in capitulation.

"Come on," snarled Hogarth, "give us that damned paper!"

He glanced over the sheet, and an even angrier snarl came from his throat.

"You must think we're crazy, young lady!" he roared. "You can go to hell before we'll sign!"

The document was not only an order for Dan's release, but a confession of the criminal manner in which he had been seized and detained.

"Better think it over, gentlemen," advised Lucile, as the prisoners continued to hold out against signing.

And this was exactly what they did. After more than twelve hours, during which they were allowed neither food nor drink (it being impossible to digest anything in a paralyzed state), the victims realized that they had no chance except to sign, or miserably to perish. And not being of the stuff of which heroes are made, they grumblingly asked the guards to deparalyze them sufficiently to let them sign the paper.

Thus it came about that Dan was again delivered from the basement prison, and that he and his wife were restored to one another's arms. Thus, thanks to his discovery and her application of it, the earth was saved from the most terrible peril in history, and gradually was brought back to its true orbit. And thus, after Dan had broadcasted all he knew about the plots of the Triumvirate, Hogarth, Wiley and Malvine were discredited and disgraced, and, deserted by their confederates, stood trial for Dan's kidnapping and imprisonment. The last that was heard of them, they were still serving their twenty-year terms at Wilmott Penitentiary.

As for the Cosmic Deflector—after the earth's orbit was righted, the secret of it was sealed in a vault at Merlin University. "I've discovered, Lucile," remarked Dan, shortly after his release, "it's not a safe invention to entrust in human hands.

"But there's one thing," he went on, as his lips moved toward hers, "if it drew the earth out of its orbit, it also drew us closer together."

Her answering smile told him that, so far as they were concerned, the Deflector had been a success.

www.ingramcontent.com/pod-product-compliance
Lightning Source LLC
Chambersburg PA
CBHW071355130626
46556CB00005B/2196